TORTOISE TALES

Dolly's Revenge

by Sheila Groves

illustrations by Gordon Stowell

KINGSWAY PUBLICATIONS

"Hmm! Not bad, not bad at all!" More-Haste-Less-Speed, as the old tortoise was called, handed his great-grandson back his end of term report. "Reading: very good progress. . . I'll tell you what," he beckoned the tiny tortoise to come closer and whispered in his ear. "Next time you come, you shall have a story of your very own!"

"Great-grandpapa!" The tiny tortoise, whose name was Take-Your-Time, couldn't believe his ears. He loved stories, especially the ones great-grandpapa told. "Really? My own for keeps?" And he jigged excitedly from one foot to the other until More-Haste-Less-Speed told him to stop it, he was getting dizzy. . .

"Not so hot on maths, though, are you? Let me see. . . 'Take-Your-Time should concentrate more on his sums and less on his neighbours'—what's all that about, then?"

Take-Your-Time stopped jigging and hung his head. "It's Easy-Does-It," he said. "He sits next to me—and he can't do maths either, so he tries to play noughts and crosses on my shell instead, or else

writes rude notes and passes them under the desk."

"And you *have* to reply, of course," said his great-grandpapa sarcastically.

"Of course!" Take-Your-Time didn't notice the sarcasm. "What else could I do?"

"Ignore him and get on with your work?" More-Haste-Less-Speed held up a paw as Take-Your-Time was about to protest. "No, you just listen a minute." And he reached for his keys, unlocked the bumpy door in his shell and drew out a leaf the colour of very milky chocolate. On the leaf a story was written. Take-Your-Time tucked his report back under his shell and settled down to listen.

Daisy and Dolly Moomuch lived in the corner of an enormous field; the corner with the old oak tree and the place where the shady, uncertain little stream decided to become a pool. Daisy and Dolly were the finest Jersey cows in the neighbourhood. Everyone thought so: the farmer, of course; and all the villagers; and the rest of the animals on the farm, even the other cows. And Buzz-Off.

His real name was Barnaby Buzz, and he was a fly. When he was little, everyone said "Oh, buzz off!" to him so often that he thought *that* was his real name—and now it was. At least, that was what everyone called him.

Buzz-Off thought Daisy and Dolly were beautiful, with their creamy brown coats, enormous brown eyes and twitchy ears. Every day he went to visit them—and he nearly drove them mad.

Buzz, buzz, buzz. . . where was he now? Perched on their noses, in and out of their ears, practically in their eyes. . . and every time they tried to catch him with a flick of their ears or a thwack of their tails, Buzz-Off would zip smartly out of reach and make rude noises.

Dolly suffered most. The minute she

heard Buzz-Off coming, she would go all of a twitch, and her mind was so full of him that she'd even forget to chew the cud and count the hours until milking time. She twisted and turned, switched and scratched, fretted and fussed, but she only grew more and more exhausted, and Buzz-Off enjoyed himself all the more.

"Take it easy, old girl!" Daisy kept saying. "Don't let him upset you so, little mischief not a fraction your size!"

"What's size got to do with it?" grumbled Dolly. "My eyes are running and my ears are sore and he makes me itch all over! I'll get him one of these days, you'll see!"

Daisy shook her head sadly. "Can't spend your life getting your own back on people," she said. "Doesn't do you or them any good—moo!"

"You're just soft," snorted Dolly, turning her back on her sister. "Let everyone walk over you, you would."

Daisy sighed, but said no more.

It was only a few days later when the accident happened. It was such a fine, hot sunny day that Buzz-Off had got up early, and made straight for the corner of the field with the oak tree and the pool and Dolly and Daisy. And ever since early milking time, he had been driving them both mad. But while Daisy was resigned

and patiently went on grazing and chewing, Dolly got madder and madder and madder.

"I'll—I'll *murder* you, you pesky little pest!" she bellowed. "I'll blow you into the middle of next week! I'll make you into squashed-fly biscuits! Take that!"

And she took a violent swipe at him with her head.

Unfortunately, she was standing at the edge of the field right next to the new barbed wire fence which the farmer had put up the week before. Her head went straight between the two strands of wire and there she was, stuck fast, not daring to move because of the spikes.

It was a long time before the farmer discovered her there, and by that time Dolly was very frightened and very subdued. Luckily, Buzz-Off seemed to have disappeared.

It took the farmer nearly an hour to get her out, because he didn't want to cut his new barbed wire, and Dolly was so scared she always pushed in the wrong direction, and so heavy that he wasn't strong enough to push her back.

"Phew!" said poor Dolly when she was finally free, her lovely coat all damp and ruffled. "I'll never bother with that silly fly again—it's not worth it!"

Daisy licked her sister's nose and nuzzled up to her.

The next morning, when Dolly was feeling better and the two sisters were taking a stroll round the oak tree, Daisy suddenly stopped.

"Look!" she nodded up into the branches of the oak tree.

It had been raining in the night, and the raindrops still shimmered on a big, lacy spider's-web, delicately stretched between two low branches. The spider was busy making fast the last corner of the

web to a twig; but it wasn't her that Daisy was looking at.

In the very middle of the web, his legs tied together and bundled up in a ball, lay Buzz-Off, very still and very silent.

Daisy and Dolly looked at each other.

"Always get what's coming to them in the end," remarked Daisy, and Dolly, stretching her poor, stiff neck, had to agree.

"I'd like to see Easy-Does-It in the middle of a spider's web," giggled Take-Your-Time.

More-Haste-Less-Speed glared at him over his spectacles.

"Whatever may or may not be coming to your young friend," he said severely, "is not for you or me to say. But when your next term's report comes out, I want to see 'Maths: excellent'!" He poked Take-Your-Time with his spectacles. "You get my point?"

It's easy to want to get your own back, isn't it?

If somebody 'borrowed' your pencil and didn't give it back, it might make you want to take something of theirs in return!

But Jesus tells us that it would be wrong to do that. He said that we must not pay back one wrong with another: we must overcome wrong things with right ones. This means that if someone hurts us in any way, we must not try to hurt them back, but to be kind to them.

This may not always seem fair; but God says that *he* will one day deal with the people who have done wrong things: it is up to him, not to us!

Text copyright © Sheila Groves 1976. Illustrations copyright © Gordon Stowell 1981. Printed in Great Britain for Kingsway Publications Ltd., Lottbridge Drove, Eastbourne BN23 6NT. All rights reserved.

Co-edition arranged with the help of Angus Hudson, London